THIS CANDLEWICK BOOK BELONGS TO:

_____

_____

_____

To Barbara, the only You Person for me
D. E.

For Savannah
R. C.

Text copyright © 2004 by David Elliott
Illustrations copyright © 2004 by Randy Cecil

First paperback edition 2009

The Library of Congress has cataloged the hardcover edition as follows:

Elliott, David.
And here's to you! / David Elliott ; illustrated by Randy Cecil. —1st ed.
p.   cm.
Summary: A rhyming celebration of all sorts of creatures, from the Feather People
(birds) to the Dreaming People (dogs) and even the People People.
ISBN 978-0-7636-1427-0 (hardcover)
[1. Animals—Fiction. 2. Birds—Fiction. 3. Stories in rhyme.]
I. Cecil, Randy, ill. II. Title.
PZ8.3.E492 He 2003
[E]—dc21   2001035063

ISBN 978-0-7636-4126-9 (paperback)

15 16 CCP 13 12 11 10 9 8 7

Printed in Shenzen, Guangdong, China

This book was typeset in Alpha.
The illustrations were done in oil on paper.

Candlewick Press
99 Dover Street
Somerville, Massachusetts 02144

visit us at www.candlewick.com

CANDLEWICK PRESS

And Here's to You!

David Elliott

illustrated by Randy Cecil

Here's to the birds!

The Feather People!

Birds!

Here's to the who-o-o ones,
The cock-a-doodle-doo ones,
Their breasts as red as fire ones,
The sitting on the wire ones.

Here's to the fish!

The Bubble People!

Fish!

Here's to the spiny ones,

The river and the briny ones,

The toothy and the eely ones,

All squishy squishy-feely ones.

Oh, I love the fish!

Here's to the bears! The Hungry People!

Bears!

Here's to the black ones,

The humps on their backs ones.

Here's to the white ones,

The swimming through the night ones.

Here's to the bugs!

The Leggy People!

Bugs!

Here's to the sting-y ones,

The weird and the wing-y ones.

Here's to the funny ones,

The buzzing making honey ones.

Oh, I love the bugs!

Here's to the cats! The Purring People!

Cats!

Here's to the creeping ones,

The get you when you're sleeping ones,

All country-wild and city ones,

The KITTY KITTY KITTY ones.

Here's to the dogs!
The Dreaming People!
Dogs!
Here's to the howling ones,
The running, yipping, yowling ones,
All go and fetch a stick ones,
The LICK LICK LICK LICK LICK ones.

Oh, I love the dogs!

Here's to the cows! The Giving People!

Cows!

Here's to the woolly ones,

The bonny and the bully ones.

Here's to the silky ones,

And butter-cream and milky ones.

Oh, I love the cows!

Here's to the frogs!

The Singing People!

Frogs!

Here's to the bass ones,

The big nothing-but-face ones.

Here's to little peeping ones,

And lily pad and leaping ones.

Here's to the people!

The People People!

People!

Here's to the merry ones,

The bald and the hairy ones.

Here's to the mom and dad ones,
And polka-dot and plaid ones.

Oh, I love the people!

And here's to you!
The You Person!
You!

Here's to the sweet you,

The messy and the neat you,

The funny-way-you-eat you,

The head to your feet you,

The bones and the meat you,

The total and complete you.

Oh, how I love you!

The You Person!

You Person You!

Yes!
You!
I love you!

David Elliott is the author of several books for children, including *The Cool Crazy Crickets*, *The Transmogrification of Roscoe Wizzle*, *On the Farm*, and the Evangeline Mudd series. About *And Here's to You!*, he says, "My neighbor's rooster and I were having a disagreement. I wanted to sleep in the morning; he wanted to crow. The rooster won, of course. The first verse of *And Here's to You!* is a tribute to his victory and to the joys found in simply following your nature." David Elliott lives in New Hampshire with his wife and son.

Randy Cecil is a graduate of the Rhode Island School of Design and has illustrated many books for children, including *One Is a Snail, Ten Is a Crab* by April Pulley Sayre and Jeff Sayre and *Looking for a Moose* by Phyllis Root. About *And Here's to You!*, he says, "It's about time that the eels and wasps got to join in on the fun with the bears and kittens!" Randy Cecil lives in Texas.